LETTING GO

Sushma Gupta

FanatiXx Publication

AM/56, Basanti Colony, Rourkela 769012, Odisha
ISO 9001:2015 CERTIFIED
Website: *www.fanatixx.in*

"LETTING GO"

By: SUSHMA GUPTA

ISBN: 978-93-89557-74-9

English Poetry

1st Edition

Price: 300.00 INR
BOOK FORMATTING: MANOGNA SRINIVAS
BOOK COVER: SAGAR SAMAL
PRESENTED BY: REASONS AND LAUGHTER

DISCLAIMER

This is a work of fiction. Our editors have tried their best to edit the content of all the author/authors and check the plagiarism. All the write-ups in this book are unique and are only published in this book.

In case any plagiarism or error is found, the author is the sole responsible and not the publisher.

ACKNOWLEDGEMENT

Compiling a book is harder than I thought and more rewarding than I could ever have imagined.

This wouldn't have been possible without the support of my friends and family.

I thank Japneet Kaur for giving me an opportunity as a compiler for Letting Go.

I extend my wishes to Reasons and Laughter & FanatiXx team for providing me with a chance to publish the work of amateur writers.

I'm forever indebted to Jonah Watts, Manogna Srinivas and Sushma Battineni for their editorial, promotional and managerial assistance.

Finally, to all the co-authors who have been a part of Letting Go. Thanks for believing and cooperating with us. Without you all this wouldn't have happened.

This anthology focuses on emotions or people that we bid good bye and let go.

COMPILER

SUSHMA GUPTA

A 21-year-old film buff lost in her own world. Her destiny made her an engineer while she ended up as a writer. A writer of melancholy and sadness who is in search of silver lining to the dark clouds. Wears the Waves of curls and has that stardust in her smile. Too lazy to move but never lazy to pen down things. Indulges if it involves food or anything she loves to do. Prefers pizza over people. Owns a pot of memories and a stack of untold Stories that would stir up rage. Lives with fire in her heart and utter chaos in her brain.

IG Handle: @sushma_guptaa

FOUNDER

JAPNEET KAUR

Japneet Kaur, daughter of Mr. Surjeet Singh and Mrs. Dilpreet Kaur was brought up in Indirapuram, UP. She is pursuing German language and BA programming course from Delhi University. She is a passionate writer who loves to pen down her emotions and environment and strive to make her parents proud.

She is even working on her very first novel, making her one step closer to her goal.

IG Handle: @sheedreamss

EDITOR

JONAH WATTS

An engineer by fate! Curiosity being his middle name, often found eating chocolates or lecturing the world about anatomy and what not. Lover of food, caffeine, pens and sleep out of the most. Believer of the notion 'pain is pleasure.' Total sucker for little things. Strong enough to let go and weak enough to look back. Procrastinates about his miseries while writing down the night and reaching for the stars.

IG Handle: @the_melancholic_writer

DESIGNER

SAGAR SAMAL

Sagar Samal is a Photographer, Image Manipulation and Colour Grading
Artist. Hardworking with a "Create Something Awesome" Mentality.
A graduate in Bachelor of Computer Application but an Artist By Heart.

IG Handle: @photosign.cf

PROMOTER

MANOGNA SRINIVAS

Manogna Srinivas of the house Hufflepuff, Hater of her Name,
Resident of abandoned window sills.
Can be found preaching about relationship turmoil while she herself
can't deal with any.
If it were up to her, monsoons would've lasted all through year.
Loves Cats and Severus equally as her Coffee and Tea.

IG Handle: @manognaa.s

MANAGER

SIVA SUSHMA BATTINENI

A twenty something with a seventy-year soul.
Often found drawing mandalas and sleeping or binge watching Grey's
Anatomy. Always wished that life came with a background score.
Gets compulsive about Dulquer Salmaan or anything related to him.
When lost, probably can be found in a corner eating chocolates.
Mountains over beaches and food over everything else.

IG Handle: @thetalkativeatom

SUSHMA GUPTA

SNUB

Have you ever been rejected?
After tasting the bitter sweetness on his tongue.
Have you ever been rejected?
After quenching his thirsty lips.
Have you ever been rejected?
After breaking your insecurities and been
naked.
Have you ever been rejected?
After filling his voids with your pheromones.
Have you ever been rejected?
After ripping your soul to pleasure him.
Have you even been rejected?

UPTURN

In the hues of dark
Amidst the painted stars
And gloomy heavens
Demons swallowed owls
Angels twirled
The town went still
It was you and me
Just you and me
Love touched the air
Lust from within
Turned him wild
Longing desire
Locked him to her
Just a Touch
perched them at odds
Choked over senses

Mourned over glee
Flame of desire
Faded stiff
Stars betrayed
Demons gave up
And bit the sky
Lust over love
Triumphed forever

JAPNEET KAUR

OLD MEMORIES

Let's become strangers again,
Let's not talk like we used to do.
Let's not think about each other's too.
Let's not shake hands again by a first glance.
Let's not share our darkest secrets while
lighting the lamps,
Let's exit from each other's life.
Let's forget who were you and I,
Let's kill the feelings buried.
Let's not make ourselves worried;
Let's become strangers again,
Let's stop reliving those old memories with
pain.

JONAH WATTS

MELANCHOLIC MELODIES

In dormant dreams I pant for you.
Through wildfires and blizzards, I walk in
search of you.
I wear you upon my skin with scars and
bruises.
Wrapped within the chamber of my heart you
lay low.
Beneath the azure blue skies I wish to hold you
close.
Distinct shadows and lost silhouettes remind
me of your cold body.
You pass out like the dark hued clouds, dark
and demure.
Your compliments and photographs make me
hold me.
You are the chapter in my book I don't mind
reminiscing.

YOU& I

Those early winter mornings; amidst the
freezing blows.
I stood there wrapped around your arms.
Your warmth felt cosy and I could literally die
in your arms.
My soul felt content.
Here I lay reminiscing those blissful memories.
Long gone are you and I still feel you around.

MANOGNA SRINIVAS

THE PRETENCE GAME

We fought again.
Blamed each other,
Yet Again.

This time it's a little different.
With blades in my heart,
And the reeks of your words,
I leave.

Saying: That I'm done.
& You do too.
But no one ever tells us the aftermath of
leaving,
About 'How To Actually Let You Go'

So,
I just assume-
That I should hate you,
So I Burn every relic
& omit all your memories.

I try-
Scratching,
With blades.
On Myself, this stubborn heart and your name.
But there's not enough rue to cure this Hue.

I pretend-
To Hate,
You, Your guts and that damned smile,
Hating the very things that I've loved.

When I'm almost done, just when I'm about to
make this pretence my truth, I see you.
And nothing else matters.
Neither the world, nor my ego or the truth.
I think of coming back to you.
But this pretence, it's damn addictive.
It made me an expert.

So I pretend-
Not to Love you,
And that it's a goodbye.
Just as I pretend to be happy with all these
thunders in my heart.

WORDS, SCARS AND 176 OTHERS

How funny it is, that Words were the ones who
let us meet and now I'm left with none since he
left?

 I saw him leave for the very first time, A Mere
Stranger Who Cuts and Writes, the kind of guy
who mails people 'compliments'.
I'd have laughed it out if you had told me then
that he would matter so much that I'd cry to
him by telling mere tales of my life.

I just wave him bye, not knowing that this
would turn into a habit.

But life really does one upon you.

After almost twice the span of years.

 I see him leave, for the very last time, he's
become the only guy whom I could ever really
Trust, that kind of guy who calls you about 176
times just to make sure you're not mad, Who'd
have thought seeing him leave could break this
shattered heart.

But now I pull back my tears not to let him see
these longing eyes or my not so subtle
heartbreak.

Just as I wave him goodbye, knowing not if I
could ever see him.

SIVA SUSHMA BATTINENI

SUNSET

Wedged between dusk and dawn, the sky
reminded me of every memory, I was holding
on to.
The sunset reminded me of something that
needed to end to begin another day.
There I found my solace in letting go, one last
good bye and the moon that accompanied as I
tried to heal the wounds.
And perhaps, if everything that ended is to
start, for the sunset is just not the end but the
beginning.

AKKALA YASWANTH VENKATA SAI KARTHIK

GONE BUT NOT FORGOTTEN

Deny me in a way to forget, Be with Your love
instead. Not to hurt, seek your heart's love
advice on right, then look at what you lost,
never try making a recap. Your dismissal made
me stronger in path, Things in life you can
never get back. Eventually, you will realize on?

JOURNEY IN TIME

A little bit of happiness, lots of love with no
regrets. My feelings will never fade away from
you; you will always be in. Happy dreams with
you love!

BLESS

Hey Doll, God blessed you with healthy
personality and beautiful nature, have your life
with wonderful memories and happiness.
I wish you that curve on your face will not fade
away.

ANUSHA DHATRI

HAPPLY, NEVER AFTER

You are the one that who lights up my
mornings;
You are the one who completes my nights and
Dawns.
Never thought that a day would come,
That you will find a reason to leave.
I became engulfed with this raging in my mind,
I just wanted to run away and hide.
You poisoned my mind,
That you always loved.
I have tried to turn it off not to care,
Yet my heart still beats your name.
It is half past the point of no return,
The tip of iceberg, the sun before dawn.
My love for you is out of world,
Let my heart hear it loud
That we are not destined for being together,
This will be my goodbye forever!

ARYAN ARORA

'B-BYE DAD'

I was angry I was mad
Or in short I will say I was sad
I would have hugged you and bid you farewell
But the only 3 words I said was
"B-bye dad"

When you were called to go back to border
I cried
You told "I am going to market" but you lied
I waited for weeks I waited for months
When I was 11 I got the news that you died

I can't tell what was going in my mind
I was only 11 and that day I felt like now my
future is blind
Stupid me! I thought that it was a game of hide
and seek
You were hidden and now I have to find

But now when you were not there I was afraid
There were many things I could have said
Now I understand that the war for you was like
a rope
And I took it lightly just like a thread

Now I am 20 and still I am sad
That day was never expected to be that bad
I would have hugged you and bid you farewell
But in anger the 3 words were

"B-bye dad"

BHAGYA LAKSHMI

GLEEFUL GOODBYE

Leaving behind bigotry and bias
And forcing my narrow mind
Into a more open lane
That welcomes people of all kinds
I bid goodbye to my old self
As I start to embrace my new self,
I felt that goodbyes can do good too.

NEVER ALONE

Coping with despair
As we inevitably
Had to say goodbye
I started to feel
The parting
Was only physical
But your scent
It never really left me
And your breath
Could still be felt steadily
And those eyes
They always seem to follow me
And your heart
It definitely belonged to me.

EPHEMERAL PARTING

We said our goodbyes
With nothing at stake
But as time passed
The longing grew enormously
Consuming us in every way
Till we were vacant inside out
It was almost like,

The goodbyes we so eagerly said
Were more of 'see you again'
And it had to happen
You and me in one place again
And suddenly I felt like
The universe subtly whispered
'You both belong together
Forever and yet again.'

The goodbyes we so eagerly said
Were more of 'see you again'
And it had to happen
You and me in one place again
And suddenly I felt like
The universe subtly whispered
'You both belong together
Forever and yet again.'

BHASKAR NAIK

MEET ME AGAIN

Sorrow of the heart
Solitude of soul
Tears of the eyes
Comes out when we distinct

My endless smile
Incredible pleasure says
Not to let you go
When I came to you

Then I'm willing to ask you
To be with me for a life time
I hope we'll meet again and again

WHEN YOU LEFT ME ALONE

My smile was scolding me
My image was laughing at me
My eyes were showing sympathy on me
When you left me alone...

My hands Will decor me
My soul Will feel good
My heart Will dance
If I meet you...

Because I Love YOU...
Until my music pauses
until my Life ends
until my dearth

BHAWANA KHETARPPAL

I LOST THE RACE

> They say love is the purest
> feeling of all,
> They say when
> everything falls,
> Love stands tall,
> Didn't happen
> in my case,
> Because I lost the race,
> I do not believe
> in love anymore,
> Because love leaves only
> Bitterness and soul,
> I don't believe in
> Love anymore.

BILAL MOHAMED ZIAUDEEN

BIPOLAR

Got up on the wrong side of the bed,
Dark shades of blue in the sky pouring down.
Sitting by the window negotiating with my
mind.
Can control my thoughts, but I can't stop
reminiscing.
Love it when you come and can't take it when
you leave.
Your smell lingers around this cell,
How your lingerie undressed from nights we
don't remember.
Arms wrapped across my waist tightly closely,
While your lips curve to kiss me at first light.
Indeed a temptress woman worth being
melancholy.
Life anchored rock bottom,
Coffee mug now turned toxic.
Voiceless wind blow between my hairs,
like my past lovers fingers caressing.
Skin hurts how I miss your feel,
had all of you, some and now none of you.
When you have everything it can't be true.
Hope someday we will meet again as perfect
strangers.
Sometimes 'Good-bye' is a second chance.

CHAITANYA PAMUNUGUNDLA

DWINDLE

The mist in the sky seems faded,
When all my anxieties and nerves started
settling down.
The lousy jibes slowly seep their way into the
night sky diminishing once forever.
Finding new side lines and making it an
audacity time and again to exploit myself now
no longer exists.
Yes it all started when I thought you could stay
for some more time.
Bringing in the morning gleam into the eyes
flashing but healthy, I could feel.
But yeah it was tough to say "GOOD BYE"
Since then that gleam I experienced stayed a
paradigm the rest of my life.
I could then realise I already said a "GOOD BYE"

UNTIL NEXT TIME

The strange tangles kept me up all the time
while I'm trying to figure out when I could
untangle.
But then your tangles seemed more significant
in a Cadillac always on the move.
The journey wasn't significant but it was going,
going through the gushes and not destined.
I just stopped and stared at the tangles which
seemed new maybe weird to me but slowly,
observing the weird became the calendar duty.
Absorbing so much that even a stranger can be
a great friend

Despite having no clue about the destiny and
the next morning, the bond grew thicker. Yes it
actually tangled up tight.
It's now so hard to even think of a "GOOD BYE"
but time didn't wait.
Things had to end with tonnes of memories
loaded to be cherished for future.
This is not the end; it's just a "GOOD BYE"!

SOUVENIR

The disguised me still didn't lose the traits, it
was searching desperately for one thing which
it can finally hold on so that the presence of a
mask wouldn't make much difference.
It was when I rediscovered thou to find a muse
the camouflage was sometimes sweet and
tricky the other times.
The ability I found in bringing the muse out is
something that I can trust upon my lifetime.
The exactamundo of what I direly wanted
slipped away few times but I tried to hold back
strong.
It shook me time and again but I never gave up
which returned to me as once in a lifetime
thing.
Something's are to be remembered and some
things are to be restored within us for a lifetime
and that's you.
I can never miss that but alas!
Every phase needs a "GOOD BYE"
But I strongly feel this bidding is one such ritual
which never ends forever.
Sometimes saying a "GOOD BYE" can make
things more strong and blissful.

SORRY NOT SORRY

Passing by a new routine finding people who
can make a big-time difference is something I
can relate to when I met you.
The strange connection which bonded us
upright is more than empathy I believe.
The beliefs and values shared commonly
between us can certainly lead us to more than
an understanding pair of minds.
Good pals are like magic, they really are not like
someone for everyone.
They are just tailor-made, one such thing is our
first farewell.
Counting on the thought that one cannot stay in
everyone's life all the time is what we figured
out.
Apparently it's a genuine friendship and it can
never fall apart. It always has little
interruptions one such thing is this "GOOD
BYE"
It means stay good even after a bye, down the
line it means stay in touch.
Our "GOOD BYE" holds thousands of memories.

GAYATRI SRI AADHIBHATLA

UNCLEAN SHEETS AND A BROKEN HEART

He chuckles at me over a coffee
And smirks that he is good in bed
He talks to me About "if sizes matter "
I would sit and feel uncomfortable
Thinking what to talk next
The inner child in me can't hog over the food
I can't eat the pineapple over the pizza
In a thought that what will he think about me ?

"A date" he said and took me to the finest
restaurant, where people talk about making
love but just head over to each other's place
over lust.
I couldn't feel anything when he mentioned
about going with the flow
I am an ocean not a river, to flow according to
my will.
My tides so powerful would hit the shore
I cannot control and it's satisfyingly unfulfilling.

Changing people like nail polish every week on
my broken nails
Ugly but feeling satisfied
In this whole lie of love
I don't feel like I am falling for you
It's not even that the next time I want to meet
you
It's like swiping left and right in real life after
every date
Living for points and appreciation

He wouldn't tell me that he would want to see
me in my pyjamas and go for a movie
But surely want to see me naked and make the
sheets unclean , throwing my broken heart

somewhere beneath the bed.
I don't know what's more broken today
Our hearts?
The idea of love?
Or our fear for commitment?

WOULD YOU MIND!

Would you mind if I asked you to stay?
When we had fights and it's always a sorry that
takes but it's me who had to say
Would you mind if I asked you to listen?
When I wasn't overreacting but I was
possessive and scared of distance
Would you mind if I asked you to show?
The little things that made you happy
When I was around but you would always feel
low
Would you mind if I ask you to give me time?
Because it is something that should be mine
Would you mind if I ask you to share?
All the little things that you do and know that I
care
Would you mind if I ask you to grow?
Older with me keeping memories in photos
Would you mind if I ask you to keep
All the little secrets and moments when I weep
Would you mind If I ask you to bear
With me because neither are perfect not you
nor me

Would you mind if I ask you to just go
Because you weren't happy with me
And I know
Would you mind if I ask you not to cheat
Because I just don't want to end like another
Girl whom you have probably dated
Would you mind if I told you
Don't ever say goodbye

HARMEET SINGH

A Silent Story

Tranquillity is appropriate
for when I describe my feelings,
Living amidst the choler of emotions,
concealed in my cerebration,
Disobedient they are at certain clips,
Their desire to announce the notions
Which makes me wonder,
Are they really placid?
Or is it the dark desponded brain of mine,
That makes me vulnerable over minute
affairs of thine.
Am I afraid of verbalising the intellections?
Which speak out loud in my mentation,
"I love thee".
The thrice of lyrics haunting me,
preventing   my thoughts to bleed
I'd say that I'm definitely afraid of the
approaching "Goodbye."
And that the opportunity on
the far-flung sky will soon fly.
But, this is a feeling I'm unable to gratify,
For when it comes to communication,
I don't think I am good at it,
And I fear that the clips of the clock
will not favour me,
Because I haven't conveyed to them
what I foresee.
And I haven't transformed
my sentiments into frequencies yet.
For when I do,
It won't be a "A Silent Story" anymore.

JACINTH ANGELINA

IN MY LONE WORLD

I used to recognise myself, funny how
reflections change.
Change is good they say but what if,
change was not.
Letting go of things, habits, people,
sure does ache a lot.
But when you lose your inner self,
that's when you know, you've truly lost
something that can't be bargained for.
I miss that old quirky me, not a care in the
world, always laughing and giggling
But one day that all changed,
I tried to cover up my void with those fake
smiles and plastered faces.
But change is all about letting go
So, it was best if I let that child go prance
around in the playground on the island
nowhere.
That was buried in my thoughts
and in my thoughts alone.

KEDAR BILAKANTI

YOU BEFORE ME

I never noticed how happy I am when I was
with you.
Hope made you gleeful, Expectations made me
awful.
Your smile made my day, Later I cried every
day.
Your amicable love made me a lunatic; later the
pain I faced was dramatic.
Your future is clear, your answer made me roll
down with tears.
Goodbyes are temporary, good memories are
everlasting.
Never let your courage down, fly high till you
reach heights.

KUSHAL GUNTURU

MY PEACEMAKER OF THE NIGHT

On the road once I stood
Thinking of what my future would be
Without you, without them, without anything
I stood on a dark road, on a gloomy day
A little pitter-patter of rain,
A little noise of the wild.
Then came a voice of familiarity
A peace that I once longed for
Now staring into my empty eyes.
Like a demon to devour me
with his bloody fangs.
I took him home
Offered him tea
Told my story of what I turned out to be.
He intently listened,
Slowly sipping his Earl grey.
The past, the things that designed me
Things that made me what I am
the dreams that were lost in the journey of my
life
The goals that were put aside for the fear of
losing.
Everything that I shared, he patiently listened.
He took a big gulp
And sat up right
Tried to speak but lost for words
He wished me luck
Rose and left
Without even saying goodbye,
Then came a knock.
The whole chaos was waiting at the door.
Spinning my life like a maelstrom
beating the very last breath of my life.

Aw! That goodbye I missed is what I longed for!
Every night I look into the dark
Praying for his return
To destroy my life with his silence
Asking him to consume me with his whispers
His cold hands on my face,
His blood-shot eyes locked with mine
My warm body craved for his cold soul
My soft skin asked for his rugged touch
I cry myself to sleep
Wishing him to comeback.
One day, then came another knock in the
middle of the night
Opened the door to find a box
A box with a vial and a letter
"Ask and thou shalt receive!
You asked so I had come
I won't be with you at all times
When you want me
Rattle the vial thrice
And close your eyes
I will be present before you
Just for the night
Once the sun shines, you won't see the face of
mine"
He turned out to be moon of my life
Visiting me in the night,
Leaving me alone at the first ray of light.
I know I cannot have him forever
But his presence is magical
He is like a dark avenger that comes at night
A ghost, a demon
Yes, a demon
My little demon
My pretty little peace maker.

Still, he appears at night
In the blink of an eye
Yet leaves me in the morning
Without even saying goodbye!

LAKSHMI KALA PATTAPAGALU

OUR GOODBYE TO YOUR GOODBYE

In the world full of silence
I was standing in my dreams
and shouting for you
only for you
asking, take back your goodbye

I could sense the night smiling at me
a girl with beautiful smile
is now no late to shed tears
awaiting here for you,
only for you
to return your goodbye

In those tears hides my voice, my love, my pain,
my patience, my care for you
can't you see?
Can't you hear?
Alright, here I closed my eyes and started
feeling the immense gloom surrounded me

Sky thunders
cool breeze blowing it's waves on
now, my voice got faded
but still I can listen to your name
and that's nowhere from my heart
only my heart in lofty

I know, you heard me
I know, you saw me
also I know you are coming for me.
Oh I found you, I can see you close
looking into your eyes,
catching your hands.

With a dense hug
my heartfelt yours and yours mine
turning faces to reality
we waved a goodbye to your "Goodbye"

MANAM SAHTHI SRI

DESIRE

> When people are showered with gifts
> from their loved ones,
> I was craving for your warmth.
> When others are going on dates
> and long drives with their loved ones,
> I'm dying to get some lone time with you.
> When people are carving their names on trees,
> I was carving your name on my wrist.
> When all you wanted was your growth
> and success, this is when I realized;
> All I ever needed was your love.

FADING HEART

> Bound by the chains of love that raised her,
> she had to give up on the love,
> which brought her out of her own misery
> and fixed her broken soul.
> Torn between choosing the cause of her birth
> and reason for her live,
> she decided to bid goodbye to this cruel world.

OUTLANDISH SOUL

> With a downhearted hope, an abandoned soul,
> and a broken heart I waited,
> for you to realise my feelings.
> Through the lonely nights and heart breaking
> silence, I survived with just a hope for your
> warmth. And this is when I realised,
> To give up on you.

MANOJ KUMAR JOGAPPAGARI

STAY

Stay!
I'm not bored of this solitude but I have found
serenity in your company.

Stay!
I'm not worried about the failure but I want you
to be a part of my success.

Stay!
I'm not scared of silence but your words make
me brave.

Stay!
I'm not sick of this suffering but your smile is
my antidote.

Stay!
I want to die at this moment but your love
keeps me alive.

Stay!
I might not be your star but you are my only
moon.

Baby stay!
Not because I love you but I don't want to lose
you.

MEGHANA SHIVANI GOGU

GOODBYE

Looking at the wall and lost in stare,
Thinking of that worst nightmare
With mascara running down my face,
Gasping for breath and peace
Thoughts started rushing...
All about you,
All about "us"
The lanes we used to hold hands and walk
The ice-cream spot we used to go just to sit and
talk
The chocolates you gave after each fight
The light that flashed out of my blanket every
night
The plans we had to cut out 80th birthday cake,
Admiring the stars with a twinkle
Smiling behind those beautiful wrinkles

After out "Goodbye", nothing seems same
How good were those days,
When I never knew reason for my smiles
How scary are these days,
When I hardly have a reason to smile
The girl who was me once upon a time,
Is tired of losing to herself,
Tired of searching her own lost presence
Tired of screaming out with silence
All those silent screams are in pain
Are now in vain
For, they are left unheard.
Her every "it's okay", is not being understood
now
Her every tear is not being wiped.
She is no longer a sulky queen

No longer a chatter box
No longer "HER"

Still...
You may see her struggle,
But you'll never see her fall
You may see her trouble,
But you'll never see her fail
You may see her fight,
But you'll never see her lose!
It may take some time...
But hurt will pass
It definitely does!
Watch the scars flying away...
Go on... Grow on!!
Just smile and blink a GOODBYE.

MOUMITA MITRA

THE UNSAID LOVE TALE

Some feelings are truly precious
Among those,
Love is one.
In my life
You came as my love.

Everything was imperfectly perfect Between us
Simple life
And no harsh words
We were really perfect for each other.

Maybe it was not liked by destiny at all
That's why problems started
Coming up.

One then two
Then three and four
Likewise problems
Continued to come up.

One was solved
Then next was ready
To create a crack
In our relationship.

We were struggling
At that time
Very much.

Maybe one-day destiny realized
We are truly made for each other
Since then our problems seemed to end
To bring back happy moments again.

Finally one day
We found happiness
Knocking our door
Once again.

Since that time we are again
Living a happy life
And it seems
We have finally said goodbye
To all our problems
That destiny had brought
In our life.

I HAVE SAID GOODBYES TO MY TEARS

My broken heart
Sought relief
But you didn't come
That day onwards
I said goodbye to my tears
Since then I have not cried for a single day
Love was enough
Still, you broke my heart
I thought you would come back
To make me laugh
But you never came back

Maybe now I have moved on
That's why when I see myself now
I could feel it's a new me
Who now neither cries
Nor feels any pain in the heart
Because since the day you are gone
I have said goodbye to my tears
And I have healed the pain
Forever.

M YOGITHA CHOWDARY

FROST BITES AND GOODBYES

Took me a summer
To stand by you and wonder,
If you meant our love forever
To end as a distant thunder.

Took me a fall
To look into your soul and wonder,
If you meant our love forever
To end like a withered flower.

Took me just a day of winter
To watch you leave me shatter,
right under the mistletoe.
And I realized that,
You meant our love forever
To end with a frosty Good bye.

NAINA KASHYAP

MONTHLY GOODBYES

I remember January being kind to me,
and so did February.

It was not until March came
along that everything seemed drab.

April weakened me,
May broke me and left
scars for June to heal,
but it had its own battles to fight.

Likewise August said,
'being overlooked is an escape',
I absconded the fleeting look of July,
and the chances of me recovering
 ran away with thirty first July.

Then came August,
with its dejected attire,
he smelled like he smoked
 too many crest fallen dreams.
But in his words I found the solidity
to venture out to September.

September smelt like
new beginnings and happy endings,
and smiled revealing his thirty-two teeth.
He promised he'd take my misery away,
and I believed him,
because my sister used to say,
people with thirty-two teeth get what they say.

November and December,
made me gaiety, let me dream,
but I won't say much about them,
because looking back now,
they still feel like a dream.

Finally, January with her unwelcoming
 gates let me enter,
 she had changed over a year.
 She walked around with a forlorn look
 and made my heart a little heavy.

(By the end of January, I abandoned my heart;
 I didn't want to take more of its weight.)

February was what I feared; hollowness.
I made some futile attempt
to get my heart back,
so he made me sit with him
 and told me a secret,
"September didn't take away your sorrow,
it just passed your miseries to me."

Months broke me,
days were too short for recovery after all,
Afternoon; is the morning a little old, and
Evening; the night still young.

September took away everything from me,
February returned it all,
and now I have this burden to live with,
that I no longer have anywhere to go at all.
All these months bid goodbyes to me

TOO SOON!

Tonight I am going to visit some graves, for my grandmother told me not to bring the dead home. I'll try to make as less noise as I can.

(The spirits in my house should not know I have abandoned them)

I'll sneak out at night, for the howling of the wolves shall cover the noises I make, for the shadow of the dark, shall cover my track. I shall bring poppy flowers with me and run the five kilometres, for I know at the end of it, I shall run out of breathe, thoughts and feelings.

(But my soul will remain.)

Cemeteries do not scare me. I have been living with the dead for a long time.

(That is why they call me half-dead.)

There won't be much to tell to the bodies in the grave only the guilt that I could have tried harder.

Tonight I'll visit the graves of the words I gave up on too soon, the half written poems, and the poems that could only float in my mind, and never touch the white pages, nor the feel of the blue ink.

I could have tried harder to finish all of them.

(But I am only known as the girl who gives up on things, words and people too soon.)

I'll count the number of stars in the sky, but we
all know there is just too many. The clock will
strike twelve and I'll have to go back, for I
know, new words will be visiting me soon.

But I just wanted you to know, the wolves I met
on the way thought you were lovely. The
shadow of the dark wanted you to know, you
are the most beautiful thing it has ever covered.

(I'm sorry I gave up on you too soon, but I've
been known to give the wrong endings to the
right things.)

PADMINI VELAMURI

ONE LAST TIME

You try to smile when you meet
For that one last time
Hopeful that you stay in touch
You feel their palms against yours
For that one last time
Those suddenly are warmer than ever
The warmth melts your heart
Your heart sighs
It's painful to let go off
With the best few people
The best few experiences
The memories made
Will always be cherished
Wishing them the best
Of what successes they deserve
You wave to them
Your smile still spread wide!

PAGADALA VAMSI KRISHNA

FORGED

> She started getting into me,
> With both my wings spread out,
> I accepted her inside me,
> She dawdled in front of me,
> She tinkled in front of me,
> She started to pretend to be unknown of me,
> But there lied the irony that my soul couldn't
> touch hers.

BREACHED

> I started penning down my pain,
> But the real pain is to accept the truth,
> That you are not beside me,
> To perceive my agony.

IMPRESSION

> Humans are reaching out to space,
> but I am still remorseful that the human in me,
> did not even outreach till you.

PAVANI BIRADAR

A FORMAL GOODBYE

Now, I don't have YOU to notice my silence, my
calmness!!
And, a crazy war of words is all what I miss
badly now!!
You made me!!
You moulded me!!
And, you broke me!!
Just let me crawl in my path now,
Bye for a while to you, 'coz my heart can't spell
"Good bye" for you!!

MY LIFE VERSUS YOU

A memory blessed with 100 years of life....
A drop of tear on the cheek as a result of my
heart overfilled with joy....
Life just happened and,
Made me feel your absence!!

I WAS SPECIAL

He always used to explain how special I was, to
him.
I took him for granted. I never explained his
place in my heart 'coz it's not my cup of tea!!
But now.....
But now, I regret that I would have told him
how much he mean to me, how much I loved
him, 'coz only at least then, he would have not
left me here alone!!

PHYSICAL PAIN – MENTAL PAIN

The joy of past....
Destiny in dreams....
If everything us just a trance,
Heart felt broken and fire!!
In the moments where memories chased me,
all I wished was to push my body in to coma!!
The moment your silence told me a good bye
note,
my heart just felt the death!

MY LOVE FOR YOU

You are hating me but, I'm loving you!!
Hating the one whom I loved once, is just not
my thing!!
I'm matured enough to know the fact that I find
my happiness in your happiness!! I mean, when
one of the eyes is in pain and crying, the other
won't laugh and party!!
Yes, we are two eyes of one soul!!
I can say you good bye solidly, but you can't just
force my heart to wish you a "good bye"!!
However, good bye my soul partner!!

PRADEEPTI SHARMA

THE LAST VISIT

As I walk past your street,
I try to revisit the past memories,
Still alive,
 In the fringes of the stoned pathways,
In the cracks of the broken walls,
On the cutlery of the baker's deli,
In the fragrance of the florist's boutique,
On the edges of that wooden bench,
In all those places,
Where we coexisted,
Celebrating our togetherness,
And vouching a forever,
But,
Alas! Surreal it is,
To the outer world,
Only my soul can feel its existence,
But,
For how long?
Is a question that baffles me,
And I close my eyes,
Feel you everywhere,
Relive the past memories,
And head towards my abode,
Alone but not lonely.
As I bid adieu,
To not these memories,
But to this life itself.
Limited days left,
To embrace my physical end.
And I wish to do it alone,
Releasing the soul of all burdens,
And inhibitions of all kinds.

Unsullied this love was,
Unsullied is this soul,
Unsullied this very existence,
And unsullied this final decision.

PRATYUSH V

LET GO AND LET BE

Let it go, people who doesn't love you to
welcome people who loves you, Let it go,
season autumn to see new leaves in the season
spring.
Let it go, your past to see your blossom future.
Let it go, others opinion to follow your own
path
Let it Go, Let it all Go!
Life is Shorter enjoy Harder!!!

PRITHVI BONTULA

SAYONARA

It's easy to say but hard to leave after that, It's easy to end
but difficult to start after that.
It's a matter of two words but the pain of two hearts.
It's not an intention but it's intensity
Before saying it there is volume but after bidding it there
is vacuum.
 It seems the racing world comes to a halt.
Relation is broken and life is shaken when one has to say
it, It is a beginning of another good day as the life never
ends with a "Good bye" it says try and try.

RAJAT SUBHRAKARMAKAR

OLD TREE AND THAT BIRD

Leaves are falling
When a sudden wind embraces that old tree,
I can hear them fall
With that cold breeze make me shiver silently.

And that little bird
Watching the last leaf fall on the ground.
Will it wait for spring?
Will that old tree hear the chirping sound?

Perhaps not, it will fly
To build its home again in somewhere else.
This old tree will wait
For that little bird to return, to be its nest.

That tree will shrivel
But with time, it has learned how to hide the
pain.
Wish I can be that Tree
Wish I can hide this heavy heart and watch you
fly away.

GOODBYE SLEEP

Moon is secretly watching me
It has covered me with veil of night.
But little did it know
My heart is awake! Oh yes.
It says good bye to sleep
To keep the nightmares away,
They make me crawl back to my shell.
And those were once your memories to keep.

SAGILI GNANESWAR REDDY

NOTHING BUT

I hear those whispers; I see those shadows.
Locked and chained I lay dead in a dark room.
Bones sore vexed and bruises so fresh.
I await for the glee that lays ahead.

UNPARALLELED

A void that could never fill.
A person so irreplaceable.
Left me behind to rest beneath the starry skies.
A love story left incomplete.

SAHITHI PRERANA

THEY SAID YOU WERE GONE

They said you were gone,
Gone forever.
Yet everything around me,
reminds me of you.
The pair of tea cup stains
on my teapoy,
brings back a thousand
conversations.
The songs playing in my gramophone,
Bring back a thousand
memories.

They said you'd never
come back, Ever again.
Yet I feel you all around me.
The hair strands on my
pillow covers,
Make me feel your warmth.
The fragrance lingering in
the rooms of my home,
Makes me feel your
presence.

They said I'd never reach you,
not in a million years.
Yet I can't get you
out of my life.
The eyeliner stains on
my mirrors,
Make me believe you're
around.
The lipstick marks on
my pens,

Keep you alive in my
Surroundings.

They said they knew it all,
But they knew nothing.
You've taken
away pieces of my soul,
and it can never be
the same again.

Keep you alive in my
Surroundings.

They said they knew it all,
But they knew nothing.
You've taken
away pieces of my soul,

SAI SARANYA VUNNAM

DUST FROM THE STARS

I've seen the dust from the stars,
fill up the sky.
It was the very time our stories
stopped by.
Together we've weaved our tales
of ardour.
Under the scorching sunlight and the
veiled moonshine.

You admired the wild rose.
I fell for the impassioned scars.
You wrote down a memory;
I made it a love song.
It was the dust from the stars, that
took us there.
It left a sparkle upon us,
showing us who we were.

Slow yet unswerving, the dawn
started creeping in.
Tinges of blue and white lost their home,
as the bright yellow let out a grin.
I held onto you, trying to breathe in;
The scent of love which now started vanishing.
Our eyes shared stories, while our hearts
started to cry.
The sky started blushing a dull pink,
But it felt like a bruise that never came by.

Your skin started to dissolve,
it resembled the golden sands.
I tried to catch hold of your face,
but our poems tangled around my hands.

I could see you recede.
I could see you leave.
But all I wanted was
the warmth of your lips,
In all the places which would
make me heave.

We met when the dark curtains fell.
We dreamed as the dawn bestowed.
We were meant to be a story,
forever among the stars.
But we parted as a memory,
alive in our hearts.

SAKETH RAMAN

FLASHBACK

> I didn't knew how much you meant to me,
> Till you gave a gap for our daily routine.
> I understood that I can't forget you easily.
> Even though You replied back to me busily,
> You're the same person to me!
> The same for whom I got attracted once,
> The same with whom I had memories,
> But, I feel like I miss you now.
> I know I can't let you go,
> I hope it won't be a goodbye,
> I believe it's just a friendly wave!!

MAHAMMAD FAYAZ

HALF TRUTH

The black sky roaring in the very evening, was
the last day we met.
My mirror laughs at me that I'm desperate
These happenings let my hometown cry
Leading to hope, you receive my good bye.

LOST

You were the one who wiped out my tears, my
sadness and made my world happy and finally
you are the one who took the happiness from
my happy world, making my life Vanish.

MY FEELINGS FOR YOU

Your warm hand on my cheeks says you are
mine. Your warm hug says that we're bonded.
Your lips on my forehead say that we are
together forever.
But we knew the day comes when we have to
move on, The day came only because of you,
So siring out with loads of dejection.

NONWIPPED FEELING

Love is a magic which gives special memories,
attention, feelings, when it comes.
But when it goes,
it gives only a feeling which can never be wiped
out.

RUINS ME

There was a time when I used to look at you and smile. But now, it's high time I ruin the same smile on your face!

67

SRAVANI KOYI

MY LAST LETTER

Before it's time for the farewell,
I'll let you go.
But in the maze of my heart,
I'm so lost.
Our parted path is just like
How the world turns to a dull tint.
If this is fated to fade away,
Then this is my last letter.
The words that I want to say- I'm writing and
rewriting them
There are so many emotions
I have towards you to let go
Knock down my Lego house
It's at the level where there's no return back to
original.
So let it be and let go.
Let's say goodbye and fly.

My days have become hectic
Just to keep myself busy.
My schedule is all filled up
Just to keep myself distracted.
But it's all of no use;
Our time together is
Burned into my brain like a tattoo.
I can't forget you
But we can't return back to our time,
So I'll take the blame
And let go.
I'm here to say goodbye...

SRITAMA BANERJEE

LOVE

She writes those dreams which are too good to
be true.
She writes to hide those feelings that she never
wanted to show.
Her pen bleeds whenever it takes his name.
It reminds her about that betrayal game.
It triggers her memories of pain.

MIRAGE

I loved you knowing my oasis
but when I came closer
You disappeared like a mirage, gifting me
nights full of nightmares.

NIGHTMARES

Sleeping on your chest was the most peaceful
place for me after mom's lap.
After every nightmare I searched for it,
 but where should I go if you became the reason
behind those nightmares??

PEN OF PAIN

I carry our memories like ink of my pain.
After you left me, it bleeds your name.

SOME UNANSWERED QUESTIONS

I can't sleep these days, only your face
comes in front of my eyes, you surely
have taken my sleep.
I can't concentrate on work,
your thoughts haunt me,
and you've taken my peace of mind.
Now please tell me,
what should I do, with this leftover heart,
which is filled with love for you??

SUMIT SAHA

FAREWELL

With the ethereal love we knit,
I see the setting sun in your eye.
Tough to say, when we'll going to meet,
Before we say goodbye.

The last silage of parting words,
That defeats me in the war,
With the tears that run from the eyes,
With cheek they shear.

Ebbing happiness, will spent times,
Trail in my breath,
I keep them in my heart,
Indelible underneath.

Ebullience in a new start,
Exuberance filled heart.
Yet a grief creeps on me,
Whispering "it's The Time To depart".

SUSHEEL BHARADWAZ

WILD AND FREE

Beneath the starry skies he stands all alone in
his solitude
Neither is there chaos in his mind nor Love in
his heart
He thought to himself "I am now wild and free"
Little did he know that he was empty from
within, All he had was a void that couldn't be
replaced by anyone else but her!

TOXICATION

The world swirled like never before,
Chaos was all that filled his cerebrum.
With every sip out of that curvy glass
his throat burned.

Yet, soothed his wounded heart
Gently it did slide through his Oesophagus
Landing flat in his empty stomach

Made him forget all his iniquities
Little did he know that he was ruining
himself once and for all.
Before, she was his addiction
and now THE FANCY BOTTLE.

TEJASWI VAJINEPALLI

MY ONE SIDED LOVE

She is the love of my life
Only person I loved after my mom,
Her smile is contagious,
Her presence is an addiction,
She is my treasure.

One day at the coffee table,
While I was engrossed in her thoughts,
She came right in front of me,
Looking deep into my eyes,
She said this should end.

She asked for a break-up,
To the reasons un-known,
I was heartbroken at hearing that,
To the core that I was lost,
Away from present.

With tears in my eyes, agony in my heart,
I asked, "Will you be happy without me?"
Without a second thought, she said "Yes"
Without a second thought, I bid her adieu.

Loving someone is not just loving their
company
True love is being able to love their happiness
Though their company might not be present
It was hard in the beginning, but when I saw
her happy,
I let go of sadness feeling proud for she is
Happy.

TULLURU SRAVANI SOWJANYA

REVOIR

Everything happens for a reason - The Apt definition of
Goodbye. Goodbye is to the person, not to the memories
you shared with him.

The saddest goodbye is when your best friend leaves
abroad to study. The one who came to you, the one who
asked you to be a friend. The one who loved you more
than you did.
She is the one who left you sooner than your shadow.
But Why?
Just hope, Sometimes goodbyes may lead to a new
journey.

VENKATESH A

FANTASY

These black hued clouds mock.
Hope glints on this gloomy day
All that remains is this,
Flickering desire that you will be
mine someday

FORLORN

With a broken heart I try to mend yours.
With melancholy inside I sing to you
lullabies.
With grief I bid you goodbye.
A painful memory, yet it sounds so good.

VIVEK AHIMAMSH KASTURI

HALF WAY ACROSS

It's unfortunate that
We can't live together.
But it is also sure that
We can't live apart.
So, we both ceased living,
Because it is not us
But the life that has to be blamed.

HAUNTING POSSIBILITIES

I wish I can turn back the time
Where we were happy.. Back then
even though we fought a lot
we could still manage to fix it.

I wish that at the end.
You, still in my arms
solving problems together
And welcome future
And at last sigh saying
WE DID IT

FLY

When I see you,
when I hear you
and even
when I leave you!

But every time I fly
It takes me another life
To come back to life.

STAY

Don't just leave yet
Look me in the eye
Whispering sweet nothings
And making me
feel special
on top of the world

Don't just leave yet
Wrap me around your arms
Spreading your warmth
comforting me with your care
Making me feel protected

Don't just leave yet
Kiss me in my palm
Making me feel loved
Like I'm only one for you
Now and forever into eternity

Don't just leave yet
My dear
Without bidding
A proper Good bye!

YANAMANDRA LAKSHMI HIMAJA

REMINISCENCE OF PAST

Sitting on the shore,
with a book in hand.
Going through those lines,
that took me to trance.
Then I closed my eyes in peace,
where the world is only you and me.
Suddenly the touch of waves
interrupted my thoughts.
My heart is filled with pride,
with the words that you scribbled.
I realized the worth behind letting you go,
real meaning of good bye,
it's between two people,
but not two hearts.
As memories keeps their story alive,
which made me feel glee,
My mind is now surrounded with positivity.

ZURI SHADDAI

FORGETTING

You think forgetting is easy-
Try not to smile when you hear her name,
Try not to remember the moments you had
when you walk past by the places you had fun.
Try not to feel nostalgic to the songs you heard
together.
Try not to expect a text from her when you
already know that she's not going to reply.
Try not to remember her voice while all you
hear is her whisperings during your sleep.
Try to be happy while you aren't alive without
the touch of her.
Finally, try spending a day without the thought
of her on your mind.

BSV SAGAR

SEE YOU LATER

They met, fought, clicked, laughed, cried, and relished every moment that was spent together until they can no longer do so. Knowing all too well that this day would come but still they held on to the last glimmer of hope, neither of them have the courage nor the intention to leave the other behind and yet they can't be together anymore. With an aching heart and lots of memories, abruptly stopping all the dreams they made for themselves, they are leaving this world which didn't understand them. Saying goodbye to each other, they took the final step hoping maybe in the next life they may see it together!!!!

THIS IS NOT THE END!

Being dubious with what he had done the previous day he fought hard not to shed the whelmed up tears, he consoled himself saying 'This is not the end!' Trying hard to forget the nostalgia which was his routine for the past years he got up from bed to start a new day, the first day after saying goodbye to each other. Even though his mind is not accepting the fact that the future where they are together is just a mirage and that it can never be true he just continued on with his day.

BENAZIR BANU

LETTING GO

Missing someone is a feeling that messes up my
heartbeats.
You leaving me, without saying a word even
if it's for my well-being.
The drifting distance between us, our diverging
horizon turns out yearnings are better than
meeting. My heart silently waits at the cliff of
firements. Things end but memories remain
unforgettable. No matter how far I will tread,
I will always keep it close.
Even though we are facing this moment of
farewell now this goodbye isn't forever and the
dazzling moments I experienced that was a
tremendous source of comfort and warmth you
were to me.
I hope this won't be too sad for you because
it doesn't mean our love is over.
Even if there comes a moment where the
longing is unbearable please get through it.
I hope my absence can be filled with laughter
and happiness rather than anger and
resentment and I hope you can replace the
anger and Fury in you with peace and
happiness.
Time will make wrinkles more beautiful!

ELLURU ANURAG

YOU

You have deserted the happiness in my life
And drowned me in the ocean of sadness.
Life became so dark, Even light has become
afraid of that darkness.
At war with my own mind every day,
Defeated in the thoughts of despair.
I Became a prisoner of the past, where I lost
myself, I've now become someone,
I don't even like.

GAGAN KOHLI

DARK LOVE

Don't leave me alone in the middle of this dark
night;
My path is full of darkness.
And I don't want to lose my source of light.
My heart is full of tears and fears,
come hug me tight.
I need you,
cause you always make me feel alright.

JAGADESH CHANDRA

ON ONE'S LONESOME

Slowly I seep into my solitude
where you no longer haunt.
Neither do my scars hurt nor are bruises sore
in pain.
Here I live in my own bubble to escape the
 inevitable reality.

NIKHIL CHAUHAN

GOODBYE, IT'S A SEE YOU LATER?

As bad as it was & hurt, we always thank God
for not getting what we thought and we
deserved.

Life will lead you down a different road, when
we're holding onto someone that we got to let
go of.

Someday we will see the reason why, &
sometimes there is good in Goodbye. Let go &
let God.

REVANTH ANISHETTI

SEE YOU SOON

When they meet each other for the one last
moment time ticks fastly,

Cloud chimes Smoothly,

Wind Whispers heavily,

They bestow their hearts to each other and stay
silent,

Their Silence is a mere of yelling good bye to
each other as on time and destiny decides their
next meeting.

VAISHNAVI BHASKARA

LET IT GO

To let go of anything unnecessary that weighs
you down is not as difficult as it seems to be.
Bidding goodbyes can make you realise this!

CO-AUTHORS

Akkala yaswanth venkata sai karthik, amateur writer from Tenali . Love making new friends and go on travel expeditions. Always up for organising events and parties. He believe in love and write about it as well.

IAnusha Dhatri , being in love and writing her whole life, she always wanted to find her own peace and happiness in her writings. This is how it started to learn from her own mistakes and step by step she started building her own empire. And let the world hear it loud and clear that she is not alone,she is always with her smile to fight for her own rights.

Aryan Arora ,a boy of small town , having big goals in mind. With full competitive spirit, Aryan Arora(S/O Mr Atul and Mrs Neetu Arora) Loves to write on any topic .It's quite strange that being a son of a grain merchant and a principal, he loves to write .His favourite place is none other than the school, St Basils school, Basti. His aim is to do something great and different from everyone else.

Bhagya Lakshmi , a girl who is a mix of an
Introvert, an Extrovert and an Ambivert.
Has a long standing affair with books and cocoa
and is often found in libraries whispering
flirtatiously to books or writing down her feelings
into verses.
An incurable romantic inside the skull but
practically lives as a nerd.
Currently focused on finding herself, looking
forward to all the places life is about to take her to!

Bhaskar Naik , pursuing
engineering . Interested to express
his feeling through words. writes
most of the thing about love and
dedicate them to his love.
Awaiting for destiny to bring back
his love for him.

Bhawana khetarppal , daughter of
Mr.veer savarkar and Mrs.kashika
lives in Roorkee. Crazy and bold girl.
She never gave up on things. She loves
challenges Crazy for food.
Believes that everyone will see her story
with her eyes, so she writes to tell
everyone the way it is.

Bilal Mohamed Ziaudeen , pursuing masters in finance. Currently residing in Kuwait.
World is a library of ideas. Ink words between a parchment sheet, bottled up with feelings. People can recite & relive a lost moment.

Chaitanya Pamunugundla who believes in spirituality to engross and manage all the physical , material, social, psychological needs of mine. Having tonnes of thoughts to express, he choose penning down things as one of the source of communication.
Not a regular writer but surely a regulator of his own life. #peaceisnottheultimate

Gayatri Sriaadhibhatla , a 21 year old girl messed up in this weird world . An environmental enthusiast who writes at times .

Harmeet singh, a Freelance Writer from Dehradun whose day commences with the vision of inditing and ends with him being glued to the silver screen. He loves to fashion the rhythmic words and centers his writings towards society. Besides, he is an admirer of allegorical romance.

Jacinth Angelina, a bangalorean heart and biotechnology engineer in making. Sucker for charms and anime.

Kedar Bilakanti , classic name with a contemporary lifestyle. Being the same engineer like most of them . Possessing Caffeinated veins all over. You find me either munching popcorn or shaking the legs on the floor. Brands over Trends , joy over everything.

Kushal Gunturu, a 19-year old gamer geek who had suddenly turned tables for the love of writing. Doctor by the day and writer by the night made him a batman for his own dreams. Sometimes you can find him wearing a flashlight to his head and constantly scribbling on pages along with serious cursing and anxiety. A perfect specimen of introvert, foodie and geek but a great writer by heart.

Lakshmi Kala Pattapagalu, A girl who started her journey towards gloom in search of light, wanted to prove that "she" can achieve anything and make impossible things to possible if one believes in oneself. Begins with self-love, self-satisfaction, encouragement, desire. She is keen to answer her past.

Manam Sahithi Sri , a lazy bug always try to enjoy doing nothing. Her soul always craves for adventures. Mostly found reading novels or gardening. Tries to fill the entire day just with sleep.

Manoj Kumar Jogappagari is from Madanapalle , Andhra Pradesh. Loves to spend time with books than people. Fond of making memes. A chai lover and an amateur writer.

Meghana Shivani Gogu, pursuing Masters of Engineering at La Trobe University, Melbourne, Australia.

Moumita Mitra is from the City of Joy, Kolkata. She has completed her post graduation in law. Inking thoughts into written words is her passion and she loves to write on any topic, anywhere, anytime.

M Yogitha Chowdary , a 20 year old food afficionado , often survives on coffee and lives in a world of butterflies. A True admirer of the cute little things in life. Her writings come alive when her emotions start to breathe.

Naina Kashyap , a blossoming teen weaving her words through her heart . Getting used to the unspoken side of teenage . A mix of shy and sass . she is just a person with kids heart and a mature pen .

Padmini Velamuri has the whole world occupying her interest. Be it weaving words together, writing a computer program, or monitoring biological reactions happening. A writer, an anchor, a biotechnologist, she proudly calls herself. Her silence defines her as to how reserved she can get. Wrap her in a bit of comfort and you'll never regret getting to know her.

Pagadala Vamsi Krishna is quite very interesting to pull people into pening down their thoughts and feelings. Someone got into writing those was a 19 year old boy who never stops acheiving. Learns everything that other people point out that he doesn't know. His heart is full of sentiments and loves to keep them to himself. Eats a lot and speaks a lot.

Pavani Biradar just had a 20 Birthday celebrations but more than required life experiences, society called her engineer but she called herself a writeup-maker. Life is her passion and putting it into words is what she loves!!

Pradeepti Sharma , a banker by profession, but loves words more than numbers. Intrigued by the fine nuances of life, like music, art, literature, and love. Loves cooking and dancing. Children make her joyful to the core. Spirituality and philosophy define her existence.

Pratyush V from City of Destiny. He would like his career to revolve around writing, which I fondly call The Art of Words!!!

Prithvi Bontula , a Liverpool fan of life.
Travel freak.
Always enthusiastic to explore new beginnings.

Rajat Subhra Karmakar, from Jalpaiguri, West Bengal, India. Currently staying in Taiwan to work as a post-doctoral researcher. Love reading and writing. Often try to write poetry.

Sagili Gnaneswar Reddy , a 21 year lad with a 60's soul. Often lectures about philosophy of life. Binge watcher of movies. I go around yoga pyramids to find peace. Caffeinated popstick. Solitude admirer of joy.

Sahithi Prerana , from the city of destiny, Visakhapatnam. she loves moonlight strolls on the shore, scented candles , fairy lights and anything that shimmers. Apart from such dreamy stuff, she abundantly love the art of writing .

Saranya Vunnam, A Biotechnologist whose thoughts lace around the ink and wander through the pages when the moon rises. Also a caffeinated soul who finds solace in the twilight hues.

Saketh Raman, from Visakhapatnam. A Post Graduation student and an aspiring writer.

Mahammad Fayaz , A 19 years old boy with hard interior who's actually not a published writer but tries to write some happenings and experiences of people on a paper. Choose profession as an engineer but just Express everything in the way he likes . Enjoys things in his own perception.

Sravani Koyi is a peripatetic introvert, lost for a while; hopelessly adrift, kept afloat, but barely, by a combination of books, a warm cup of coffee, music and pretending the world is spinning in slow motion.

Sritama Banerjee from kolkata, West Bengal. A Physics teacher of an ISC school. Love to write, read story books, sketch and dance. An admin of two Facebook pages and often try to write poetry.

Sumit Saha an 18years old guy who is preparing for his SSB interview. He wants to become an Army Officer. He loves to share his feeling through his poems. And loves to write and fight with his hands.
He is mad for playing cricket and kabaddi.

Susheel Bharadwaz pursuing Batchelor of Computers to fit in the corporate IT world. Introvert admist of extrovert mates. Food, movies, pubg over everything.

Tejaswi Vajinepalli is a published writer and a motivational speaker. He is an avid reader and a passionate writer. Currently employed in IT Industry and based out of Chennai. He loves to express himself through his words.

Tulluru Sravani Sowjanya who live in Hyderabad . Currently working in an MNC.
she completed her graduation in Mechanical Engineering. A person who tries hard until and unless she achieve something. will always try to make people around me happy.

Venkatesh A , learning the ropes of agriculture. A connoisseur of food. Spend most of his day doing nothing. Being an amateur cook, Love to make hearty meal for himself. Exploring newbies will always be on his list.

Vivek Abimamsh Kasturi , a twenty year old boy who believes in the phrases "Pen is mightier than a sword" and "Don't judge a book by it's cover". The one who tries to make sure that his writeups are stronger than the coffee he sips. He's engineer by choice which he always regrets for!He is someone who's always in search for the ray of hope!

Yanamandra Lakshmi Himaja ,completed her graduation in the stream computer science engineering. Worked in banking sector for few months and currently planning to write a book. Loves to read novels and pen down her thoughts through her blog pensive writings. Her interest on writing turned to love only because of your quotes app, where she started expressing her ideas. Mostly introvert.

Zuri shaddai, a guy with weird name in a normal city and what else will he would be doing rather than Engineering

BSV.Sagar , a techno mechi currently residing in Chennai. An anime enthusiast and an avid reader. Likes to travel and love machines.

Benazir Banu is a student by profession.she just express her inner thoughts in a piece of paper and motivate herself during her free time.

Elluru Anurag is currently pursuing his final year of BBA at Vignan University, Guntur.
He is a person who loves cycling, trekking, travelling .His mother is his role model and wants to be a civil servant. And his favourite quote is "Hope for the best but be prepared for the worst"

Gagan Kohli from Delhi, working as an IT engineer for Infosys, Chandigarh. He does poetry to express his feelings. Love to travel and click photographs.

Jagadesh Chandra humorous by soul and generous by heart. Trying to be earth's best friend. Agriculture enthusiast being tutored in the same. A procrastinator just binged into gaming. Family over everything.

Nikhil Chauhan, a 19 year old chap pursuing bachelors in the field of IT. Living, Loving and Minding his business. He is passionate about everything that he does, ranging from playing cricket to his interest in poetry. His dreams are genuine and doesn't want to be the one who follows the pack of wolves and want to become a writer and publish his poems.

Revanth Anishetti an undergrad Biotechnologist. He's a travel freak and love to explore places. He's a reality believer rather than a day dreamer. Jack of all traders , master of some. His love for music helps to delve into imaginary world.

Vaishnavi Bhaskara, a loquacious girl. She is in if there is some art campaign. Someone more interested in socializing. An avid reader of novels and a binge watcher. All hail to Friends, Food and Fun.

ABOUT REASONS AND LAUGHTER

Reasons and Laughter is a community which deals with providing services, compiling anthologies, organising competitions and Open Mics, found by Japneet Kaur.

Our main objective is to give a good platform to budding writers to help them grow, even to provide best services and giving wings to their dreams.

Email: ralservicess@gmail.com

IG Handle: @reasons_and_laughter

www.ingramcontent.com/pod-product-compliance
Lightning Source LLC
Chambersburg PA
CBHW020350160726
47987CB00022BA/2487